The Raindrops
In The Bay

Welcome to
Little Apple

Written and Illustrated By Glenn McLernon

Stuck in the slippery, slimy muck; oh yuck!
The Raindrops seemed to have run out of luck.
Then along came the tide to give them a ride,
away down the river to the big ocean wide.

As the water began to rise,
the Raindrops could hardly believe their eyes.
And so they began to float.
Their old branch was again like a boat.

At last the Raindrops were free,
floating on their branch of a tree.
They were singing a song as they drifted along,
on their way back down to the sea.

Now there were houses along the way;
excited children, all busy at play.
Gardens with flowers and plants and trees,
people sunbathing with knobbly knees.

There were trucks and buses and cars all around.
All of them making a right rowdy sound.
The Raindrops were frightened, they started to shiver.
All they had known... was the quiet of the river.

"Oh, goodness." Said Puddle.
"Just look now, there's trouble.
Those bottles and rubbish and things."
"It's people." Said Piddle.
"Too lazy." said Diddle,
"To put all their rubbish in bins."

The noise got louder as they went along.
Then Puddle could smell a terrible pong.
Were the Raindrops having a very bad dream
or was this old river much cleaner upstream?

The Raindrops hoisted a flag that read...

You know that clean land and clean rivers are best.
Take your rubbish home and don't be a pest.

The river was wide as they passed the docks.
A ship was tied up with its cargo of socks.
The captain's name was old Joey Fox.
He was born and raised in a place called Fort Knox.

From high on the deck of the ship full of socks,
somebody threw a bucket of slops.
It was slime and food waste and some terrible muck
that fell on a poor little innocent duck.

"Look out." Said Puddle.
"Some mighty big trouble.
A huge ship is coming our way."
"Quick now." Said Piddle.
"Let's hurry," said Diddle
"or we'll never get out of this bay."

The big ship went by and the waves rolled high.
The Raindrops were thrown all around.
They clung to their stick.
They were all feeling sick
and then there was hardly a sound.

Always looking around for food;
the swooping seagulls were very rude.
One of them had an odd kind of wish;
that a Raindrop would make a very tasty dish.

A Seagull swooped down! Suddenly Puddle was gone!
Pecked up by the gull who was now on the run.
The others looked-on as their poor little friend
was surely coming to a grisly end.

Puddle told a joke. It was really daft.
But the greedy seagull burst into a laugh.
Puddle escaped in the middle of this giggle
and fell back down to Piddle and Diddle.

Diddle spied something beginning with L.
It was surely a lighthouse and not some big bell.
They were near to the sea now, not far to go.
But they seemed to be going so very, very slow.

"I know why." Said Piddle.
"It's a thing called the tide,
playing its game: a twice a day ride.
It is pushing us back from where we should be,
pushing us back, away from the sea."

The tide pushed them right back into the bay,
where they would stay for the rest of the day.
The open sea was well out of reach.
Now they were floating by a sandy beach.

Pinchy crabs were playing hide-and-seek.
Seaweed and shellfish were ready to sleep.
A happy seal played beneath the setting sun.
Oh, life by the shore can be such fun.

The sun went down at the end of day.
Lights were flickering around the bay
and away out there the lighthouse beamed;
around and around so it could be seen.

Wavelets lapped gently by the shore.
The Raindrops fell asleep and one of them snored.
A foghorn sounded a gloomy hummm;
a warning to sailors that a fog had come.

"Wake up." Cried Piddle.
"What's is it?" Said Diddle
and Puddle gave out a loud shout.
"The tide has turned. It is going back out,
back out to sea, without a doubt."

The sun came up, right over the bay.
Now there was nothing at all in their way.
A school of dolphins swam by their side,
leaping for joy with the ebbing tide.

The Raindrops looked around at this wonderful sight.
Of the bay in the sunshine with people flying kites.
Of birds of the shore and birds of the land
and all around; a golden sand.

As they were heading away out to sea,
high on the cliff; someone shouted. "It's me".
Why! It was old Bungie Boo there along with McNat,
that clever and loveable, smart little cat.

Riding the waves on their branch of a tree;
the Raindrops were floating away out to sea.
Smaller and smaller and smaller they got,
until they were just a tiny little dot.

So goodbye to the river, the bay and the land.
Hello big sea with its basement of sand.
The Raindrops were finally back on the sea
It is, after-all, where they wanted to be.

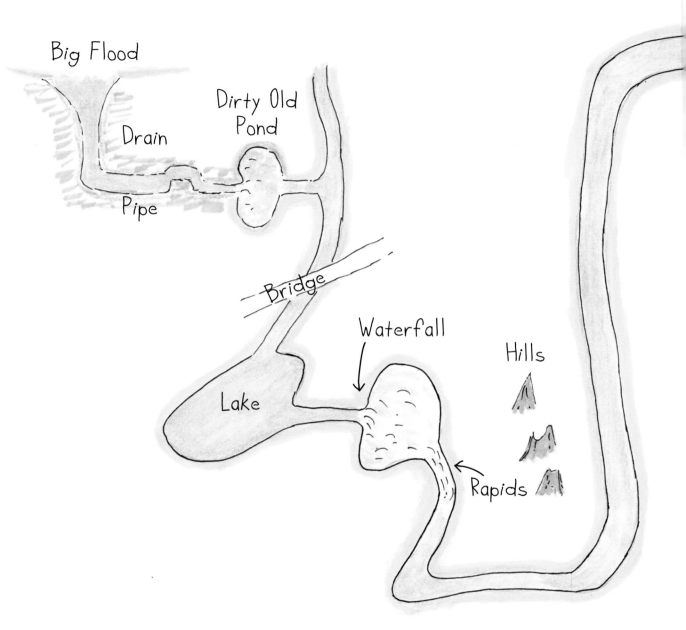

Did you see the birds as they went along?
Remember the rubbish and that terrible pong.
But don't despair. We can all do our bit.
Put you rubbish in the bin and don't be a twit.

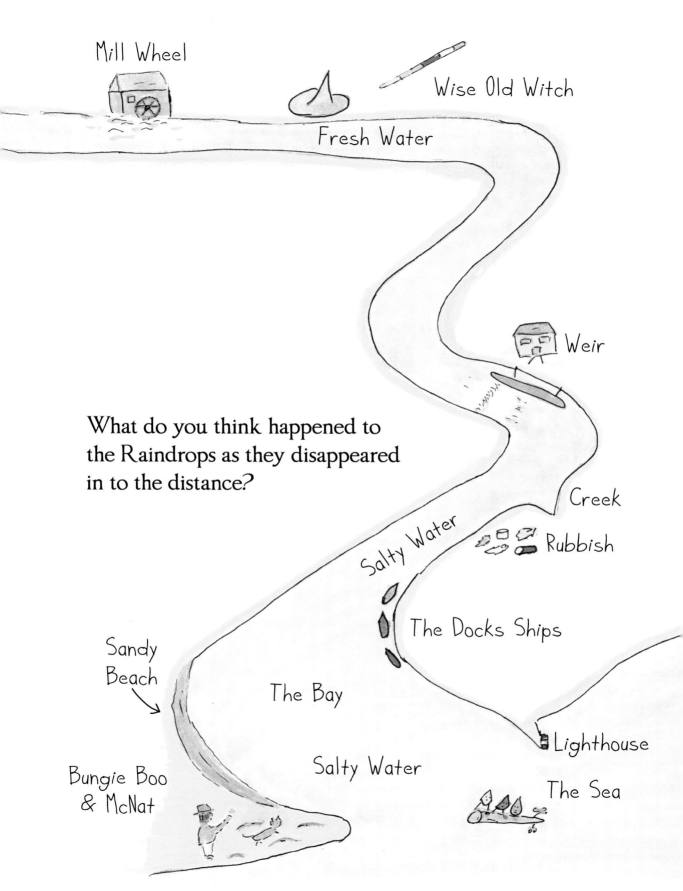

Mill Wheel

Wise Old Witch

Fresh Water

What do you think happened to
the Raindrops as they disappeared
in to the distance?

Weir

Creek

Salty Water

Rubbish

The Docks Ships

Sandy
Beach

The Bay

Lighthouse

Salty Water

Bungie Boo
& McNat

The Sea

So there you are and there you have it and that's what it's all about.

And so the Raindrops finally reached the
open sea. What might happen to them now?
Could there be further adventures for them? Maybe.

Watch out for Book 6: Snow Dance,
as the Raindrops come back as snowflakes.

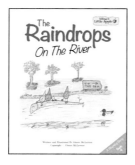

Stories from Little Apple

With thanks to Sue for her thoughts and advice during the creation
of my books. The Little Apple stories are a collaboration by
Glenn McLernon and Lorraine Harvey

The Raindrops: In the Bay

First published in 2018 by Glenn McLernon
Phone: 07503184650 (UK)
e.mail: gmclernon@googlemail.com

ISBN: 978-0-9929145-4-7

A catalogue record of this book is available from the British Library.